One Duck

Story by
Hazel Hutchins

Illustrations by
Ruth Ohi

Annick Press
Toronto • New York • Vancouver

THE CANADA COUNCIL | LE CONSEIL DES ARTS
FOR THE ARTS | DU CANADA
SINCE 1957 | DEPUIS 1957

We acknowledge the support of the Canada Council
for the Arts for our publishing program. We also thank
the Ontario Arts Council.

Cataloguing in Publication Data
Hutchins, H.J. (Hazel J.)
    One duck

ISBN 1-55037-561-X (bound) ISBN 1-55037-560-1 (pbk.)

I. Ohi, Ruth. II. Title.

PS8565.U826O53 1999   jC813'.54   C98-931958-X
PZ7.H87On 1999

The art in this book was rendered in watercolours.
The text was typeset in New Baskerville.

Distributed in Canada by:
Firefly Books Ltd.
3680 Victoria Park Avenue
Willowdale, ON
M2H 3K1

Published in the U.S.A. by Annick Press (U.S.) Ltd.
Distributed in the U.S.A. by:
Firefly Books (U.S.) Inc.
P.O. Box 1338
Ellicott Station
Buffalo, NY 14205

Printed and bound in Canada by
Friesens, Altona, Manitoba.

Dedicated to farmers,
like my dad and mom,
and with very special thanks to Tom.

One duck
at first light
feeds on a prairie pond.
Feeds only briefly
lifts from the smooth water
flies low
to the stubble field close by
circles
lands.

Hidden perfectly in a hollow of ground
down-lined, down-covered, still warm
one nest with twelve olive eggs.
Her nest.
Her eggs.
Settles down upon them
knowing it is almost time
and waits.

One farmer
at sunrise
stops to watch the sky.
One small cloud on the horizon.
Thinks about the day.
Cultivator to hook up and pull onto the stubble field
to till the soil for the wheat he'll plant and tend
and sell to feed and clothe
his family
four children
still asleep upstairs.

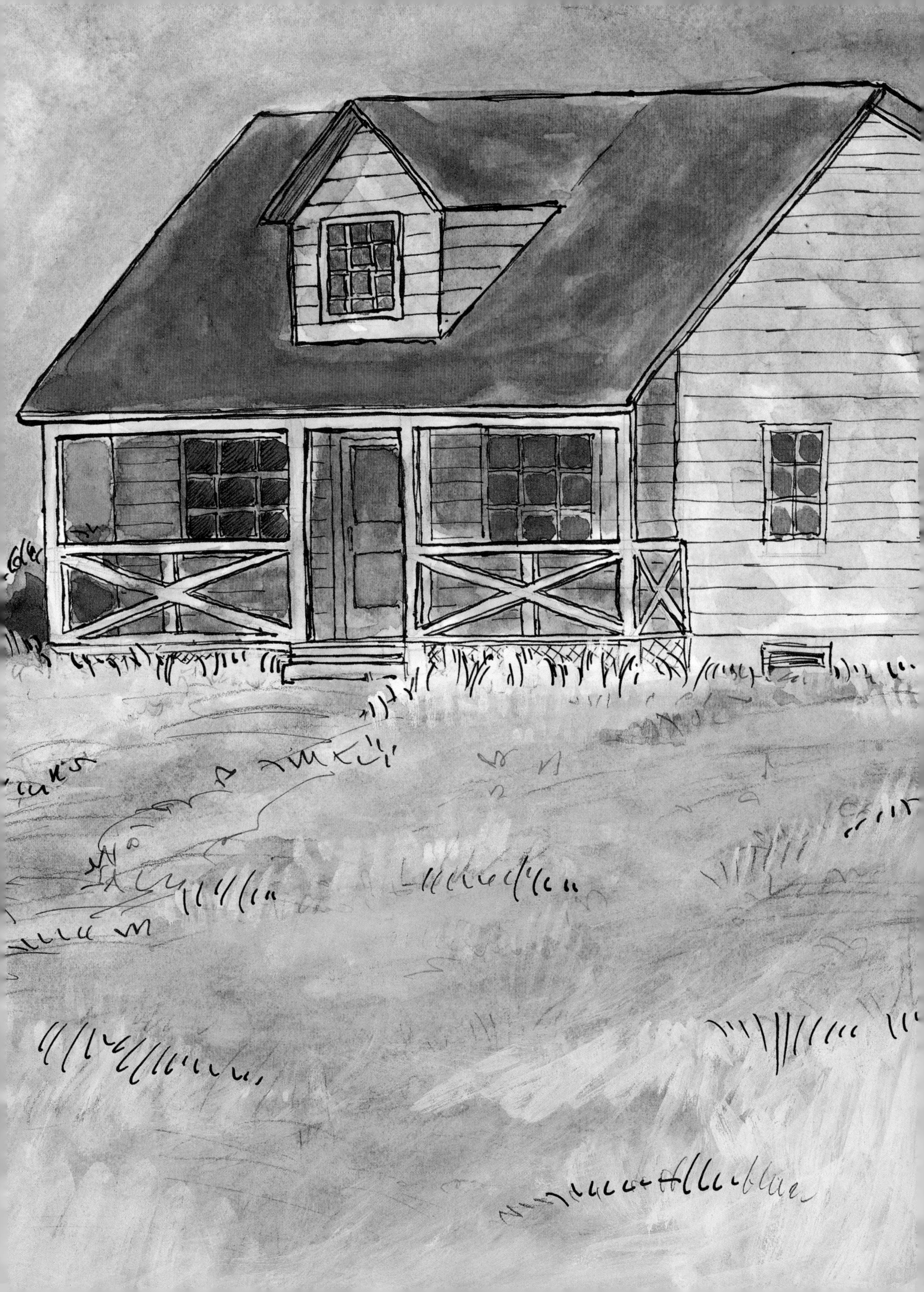

The tractor roars.
The children tumble down to breakfast
oldest helping youngest
clothes and chores and books
and a run for the school bus
just in time to wave as the farmer moves
    onto the land.
Along the outermost edge of the field
he drives the tractor.
Slowly, steadily, the cultivator cuts and
    lifts and turns the soil
the first row of a pattern leading
ever inward
towards ...

One duck
on twelve eggs.
She hears the tractor
stretches her long neck to see what can be seen
feels an uneasiness she cannot explain.
Watches.
Waits.

A crow passing overhead
looks down and sees her craning neck
guesses she has eggs to care for
alights before her
taunts and teases
scolds and flaps
torments her any way he can
tries to lure her from the nest
so he can eat the eggs.

One duck
still sits
too smart for crow tricks
watches close his wily ways
both of them too busy to notice
the tractor on its second pass around the field.

The third pass is closer still
and the fourth pass, closest of all
is a sudden wall of loudness, fumes and rolling dust
that sends the crow fleeing.

But one duck
still sits
though somewhere in her duck-brain
a single thought is clamouring—danger.

The tractor motor lessens to an idle.
The farmer swings down from his seat,
    wipes his brow
checks the tractor, checks the hitch
checks the sky.
The little cloud is building
darkening into thunderclouds
moving towards the farm
but if he hurries he can still finish
    before the rain.

The tractor roars louder now.
The farmer turns onto the row
where ...

One duck
still sits.
She sees, she hears, she feels
    the great machinery moving
closer, ever closer
and still she sits
feels the pull of the eggs beneath her
feels the danger moving down upon her.
Eggs! Danger! Eggs! Danger!
heartbeat upon heartbeat
no way to save the eggs
no way but to save herself.
She flies!

And in the split second that he sees her
the farmer knows
one duck's secret.

Almost without thinking
he stops the tractor.
He scowls but does not start up again.
He climbs down
and there before the tractor wheel finds
twelve eggs exposed to the sun
and the rain
and the crows
and the blades of the cultivator.
He shakes his head at the foolishness
    of ducks.
He checks the darkening sky
and shakes his head at the foolishness
    of farmers.

Reaches down with big hands
careful not to touch the eggs
feels the earth cool on the backs
    of his hands
feels the warmth of life
    within his cupped palms
lifts the downy tangle.
Carries it ... where?
Not too far or the mother will never
    find it again.
One row over
lays it down on land already turned
climbs back upon the tractor seat
drives away.

Crow, circling overhead
caws in great delight.
Eggs! Eggs!
Drops on bent, black wings
to glorious feast.
But one duck glides in low beneath him
just in time.

Robbed! Robbed! Robbed! cries the crow
just as the storm breaks.

One day later
when the rain has stopped
and the land has dried enough
    to work the soil
the farmer moves again into the field
    to finish up.
The afternoon sunlight grows warm
    and warmer
the final rows are done at last
and the school bus, on its homeward pass
drops the children in the lane.
The farmer stops to greet them
and the youngest child points out ...

One duck
waddling over the stubble field
followed by
twelve ducklings
crossing the road
sliding into the safety of the pond
just doing what ducks do—
one duck.

Other books by Hazel Hutchins and Ruth Ohi:

And You Can Be The Cat
The Catfish Palace
Yancy & Bear
It's Raining, Yancy & Bear
Katie's Babbling Brother
Nicholas at the Library
Norman's Snowball
Tess